Goldilocks III

by Jan Fields

illustrated by Andreas von Cotta-Schønberg

Table of Contents

Chapter 1
Prankenstein

In the 21st century, the search for habitable planets began. On these planets, where conditions were just right, Earth colonies appeared.

Colonists on new worlds have to expect the unexpected. Still, a lot had been going wrong in the colony on Goldilocks III lately. There was the alien invasion hoax and the textile-eating fungus hoax. (That one appeared on a few key victims as interesting peek-a-boo fashions.) Then, during his monthly televised speech, the colony governor was replaced on screen by a giant rat.

The source of all these pranks was the same.

Boxer Brown knew that colony life depended on everyone doing his job for the good of the whole. He knew that good colonists were good cogs in the machine. Unfortunately, Boxer Brown did not enjoy being a cog.

In Boxer's experience, being a good cog usually meant being assigned odious labor tasks. Boxer faced the labor screen and thrust his hand onto the recognition pad. "Please. No more poop," he muttered under his breath.

A key-card slid out of the slot and his assignment popped up on the screen: "Maintenance—Clean Cages, Science Pod."

"No!" Boxer committed a level two Language Decency Violation and slammed a fist on the pad.

"Hey! If you break that, I gotta fix it."

Boxer spun to face Link Reese. "At least you're not on cleanup duty in the Science Pod."

Link shrugged. "If you don't like it, transfer."

"I've tried," Boxer snarled. "For a month. They're punishing me for a few pranks they **think** I did."

Link grinned. "Everyone knows you did that stuff. The rat morph was epic!"

"And it landed me on poop patrol!" said Boxer. "I have to get out of there. I want to use my brain, not scrub cages."

Link leaned forward and dropped his voice. "I might be able to help. I can remove the punishment block from the system. But remember, failing any academic class will stop that transfer. I can't change that."

Great. Boxer was an hour away from flunking the Alien Bio midterm exam. Then an idea bloomed.

"You do your part," Boxer told Link, "and I'll do mine."

Chapter 2

Alien Lab Creatures

Boxer used his key-card to get into the zoology lab.
"Dr. Archer? Anyone?"

On normal days, there was always someone supervising the lab. But today was not a normal day. It was freak-hunting day. (Okay, Specimen Collection Day, if you wanted to be official about it.) The scientists were all outside and wouldn't be back with their new creepy crawlies for hours.

Boxer looked around. If he could get in a single night of cramming for Alien Bio, he would be fine. He just needed a tiny disruption to postpone the test—something that wouldn't look like a prank.

He looked at a row of cages and shuddered. The natives of Goldilocks III tended toward small and slimy. It was enough to make a guy glad that the whole colony was one big collection of pods and corridors—the outside never got in.

He poked the cages and the creatures hissed at him. Then he heard a squeak from a knee-level cage. He knelt down. Two practically-slime-free creatures with big eyes peered back at him.

Perfect! Boxer grabbed the cage.

Boxer skidded into Alien Biology with no time to spare. "Mr. Stanton, I brought something for extra credit."

Mr. Stanton was busy with a big pile of papers. "Please, take your seat for the exam."

"Okay, but you have to see these guys." Boxer plunked the cage in the middle of Mr. Stanton's desk. "Actual aliens for Alien Biology class!"

Mr. Stanton peered at the creatures with interest. "These animals are the natives on Goldilocks III, Mr. Brown. We are the aliens. Has the lab classified this species as harmless?"

"Look at the little guys," Boxer said. "Of course they're harmless."

The creatures in the cage tilted their heads adorably. The way their mouths turned up a little on their long muzzles almost looked like a smile.

With a sigh, Mr. Stanton flapped a hand toward the cage. "Bring them on another day. We have an exam to take."

"Okay." Boxer reached for the cage, and as he did, he "accidentally" flipped the latch on the door. When the door swung open, the small creatures wasted no time scurrying out. Then they surprised Boxer by unfolding wings and flying.

The class went wild, shouting and laughing. Maxwell Carter snatched a creature out of the air. He immediately yelped as the little thing sank needle-sharp teeth into his hand.

Max shook the creature off his hand while committing a Language Decency Violation that approached level four. Then his eyes rolled up and he crumpled to the floor.

"No one touch those creatures!" Mr. Stanton yelled. But it was too late.

Chapter 3
Transformation

The flyers began dive-bombing, biting anyone they could. They acted hungry—or rabid. Kids dropped like sacks of hydro-grain. The few unbitten ones raced for the hallway. So did the flyers.

Boxer dragged convulsing kids away from the desks so they wouldn't knock their heads against the legs.

"Are you okay?" Mr. Stanton was helping Max sit up. Letting out a whoosh of relieved breath, Boxer started toward them. Maybe this wouldn't be so bad after all.

He stopped when he heard Max growl.

"Maxwell, what's wrong?" Mr. Stanton asked.

Max raised his head and Boxer froze. Blood ran from the kid's eyes like tears.

That couldn't be good.

Max turned and snapped at Mr. Stanton, catching the shoulder of the teacher's enviro-suit. Luckily, no one in the colony had clothes that fit right and Max just came away with a mouthful of loose fabric. Mr. Stanton scooted backward—fast.

Max followed him. And Max was faster. He was biting into Mr. Stanton's calf when Boxer ran over and rammed Max hard, knocking him into a row of desks. Mr. Stanton made it to his feet before he started convulsing.

Boxer turned and raced for the classroom door. He was nearly there when something caught at the loose fabric of his pant leg. It was teeth.

Specifically, it was the teeth of the normally gorgeous Abigail Method. Looking at those bloody eyes and the hungry way she chewed on his pants, Boxer no longer felt any urge to ask her out. He jerked his leg away, leaving her with a mouthful of cloth.

Things weren't a lot better in the corridor. Kids and teachers lay on the floor convulsing. The few that were up looked ferocious and *ravenous*. A bite from the flyers had turned them into creatures with an appetite.

Boxer took the route that had more people on the floor and fewer looking for a lunch buddy. He jumped over a sprawled teacher. She snapped at him but missed.

He skidded around a corner to the next corridor and spotted a cluster of kids dragging someone down. "Hey!" he yelled.

Every head snapped up. Every red eye looked straight at him.

"Right, no heroics," he said as he backed away. In a bend of the corridor, something grabbed him by the arm and jerked him into one of the data alcoves.

He tried to twist away but a voice whispered in his ear. "Be still and be quiet!" It was a girl's voice. Since she wasn't biting, he obeyed. He watched as a stampede of red-eyed students raced by without a glance.

"Why didn't they come in here and eat us?" Boxer whispered.

"Not sure." This came from Sophie Masters, the second hottest girl in the colony. Considering she wasn't dripping blood, Boxer quickly moved her up in the rankings.

Link Reese stood nearby, half supported by the alcove wall. "The low-level standby energy of the communication node must somehow be cloaking us."

"We used the comm to contact security," Sophia said. "What do we do now?"

Boxer took a deep breath. "I have an idea."

Chapter 4

We Need a Hero

Sophie crossed her arms over her chest. "You want us to go all the way to the science pod?"

"The labs there can be sealed," Boxer whispered. "We have to get out of the school pod and into lockdown."

Sophie looked at Link and he shrugged. "I don't have a better plan. But I can't move too fast. I did something to my ankle."

Boxer looked down at Link's foot. "You're not going red-eye on us, are you?"

Link shook his head. "It's sprained, not bitten."

Finally Sophie said. "Okay, you lead and I'll help Link. Maybe the biologists can fix this."

"Not likely," Boxer said, peeking around the corner, "considering they're all outside."

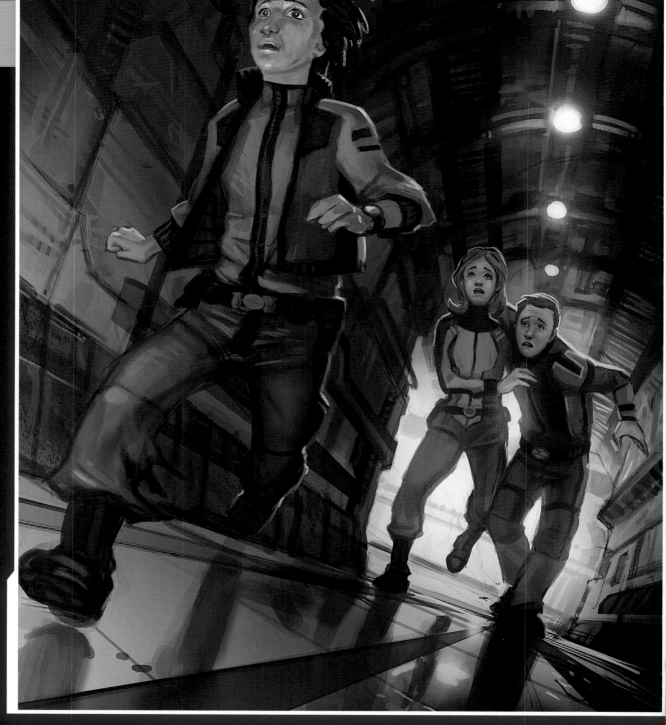

"Fantastic," Sophie muttered, but she put her arm around Link to help him upright.

Boxer sprinted for the next alcove. Sophie and Link moved slower but they made it. The trip through the school corridors and into the long junction between the school and science pods was painfully slow. Twice they had to wait and let Link rest. He was looking gray and sweaty. When they finally got into the lab, Sophie helped Link slide to the floor.

Boxer triggered the lockdown and leaned against the door. Suddenly they heard a crackle of static and a voice Boxer recognized.

"Can anyone hear me?"

"Dr. Archer? This is Boxer."

"Boxer," Dr. Archer said, relief thick in his voice. "We're back from specimen collection, but no one seems to be manning the entry doors to let us in. The oxygen won't last much longer in these breathers. What's going on?"

"Some lab animals got out," Boxer said. "Their bite is making people go crazy. Lots of people."

"Can you come and let us in?" the doctor asked.

Good question. The colony was constructed of a number of pods, each with a set of rooms. The pods were connected by long corridors. The outside access was two pods and a whole lot of corridor away from the lab. Boxer peered out the thick viewport in the door.

"It's clear so far...." he said, and then yelped when a bloody-eyed face slammed into the port. "I take that back. Not clear."

Dr. Archer's voice spoke from the comm. "I might be able to find out what's happening to everyone. But we have to get in."

"Why hasn't security arrived?" Sophie wailed.

Boxer spotted a red uniform through the door. The security guy had bloody eyes and a bite on his neck. "They are here," he said. "This is spreading *fast*." The flyers must have moved well beyond the school pod by now.

"I have an idea," Link said. "There's an atmosphere failsafe that can flood the colony with knock-out gas. I helped install it after the food riots."

Dr. Archer's response was immediate. "Can you access it from the lab?"

"I'd need an engineering node."

"Can you reach one?" Dr. Archer asked.

Link shook his head. "I can't even stand up."

Chapter 5
Mazes Are Fun...

Boxer looked back at the door port. More bloody-eyed faces snarled and snapped.

Leaving the lab was crazy. On the other hand, staying there wasn't doing any good. And this little problem was his fault.

"I'll go." He opened a drawer and pulled out an emergency breather. He'd need it for when the gas took effect.

"First we have to clear the door," Link said, pointing. "Unless someone wants to volunteer to be lunch."

Sophia looked thoughtful. "They are acting awfully hungry...." She walked over to look at the data port. "We could send a huge food dump from food services to the science lounge. It should overwhelm the serving mechanism and spill hot, good-smelling food onto the tables. That might draw our hungry friends away."

"If they eat something besides people," Boxer said.

"They do!" Link told them. "One of them ate my lunch, bag and all."

Sophie's fingers flew over the controls, while Link explained what Boxer needed to do.

"The gas won't knock them out instantly," Link warned.

"Maybe the food will keep them busy until it kicks in," Boxer said.

"Maybe."

Finally Sophia yelled, "Got it; the food is coming!"

Boxer rushed to the door and watched for the port to clear. At first, the mob went wild at the sight of Boxer on the other side of the glass. Then they caught the scent of food, and they ran toward the lounge.

"I'll send food dumps to other lounges along your route," Sophia said.

"Thanks." Boxer punched in the code to release the lockdown. The door slid open and he darted into the hall.

He could hear fighting from the lounge end of the corridor. He sprinted in the opposite direction. The engineering node was near the long corridor joining this pod with one of the housing pods. Yes! The way was clear.

Boxer snapped open the access panel of the engineering node and his fingers hurried through the steps Link had told him. When he reached the last step, typing in the security code, he risked a glance behind him.

Food-stained people were drifting from the lounge into the hallway. "Fannn...tastic," he whispered. He turned back to type in the code and his mind went blank. Were the last two digits fifty-one or sixty-one? He looked back again. The mob was closer.

The colonists spotted him then. A howl rang through the hall.

Chapter 6
...Unless You're the Cheese

"Think, think, think." Boxer didn't have time to go through the whole code again. He'd just have to take his chances. He keyed in fifty-one and slammed the entry button.

With a hiss, gas started pouring into the corridor. Boxer shoved the breather between his teeth and headed down another corridor toward the next pod and, beyond that, the entry hatch. He had to let those scientists in. A chorus of growls followed him, but he didn't look back. He just had to stay ahead of them until they passed out.

He slammed his hand into the access panel to open the doors to the next pod. Inside, a crash echoed from an open lounge to his left—one of Sophia's food dumps. He raced past without a look, hoping the bloody-eyed diners chasing him would go for the food.

The continuing growls told him that at least some had stayed on his trail. As he pounded down the halls that ran through the pod, Boxer's lungs screamed for more air than he could pull in through the breather.

The growling sounded closer. *Fall asleep, already!* He risked a desperate look behind him, then wished he hadn't.

Last pod! He was almost there. He nearly stumbled through the pod doors as they opened.

In front of him, five red-eyed security men came out of the pod's lounge. Oh, good. Trained fighters. He hoped they were too full to want dessert. They looked a little wobbly. Maybe he could run back the way he'd come, just until they dropped from the gas.

Boxer turned, just as the colonists who'd been chasing him came around a corner. One shook his head and leaned against the wall, but the others staggered on. Boxer looked desperately between the two groups. He was trapped.

Boxer made up his mind. He sucked a gulp of air through the breather and ran full tilt toward the drowsy security guys.

At the last second, he hit the floor and let his momentum carry him in a slide right between the legs of the guy in the middle.

On his feet again, he made the last curve to the outside door hatch. Outside, four scientists with breathers of their own pounded on the portal.

Boxer grinned. He was going to make it. He stepped over a slumped figure that lay still on the floor near the door controls. *About time the gas knocked someone out!*

Suddenly, the man rose up and sank his teeth deeply into Boxer's leg before falling back to the floor.

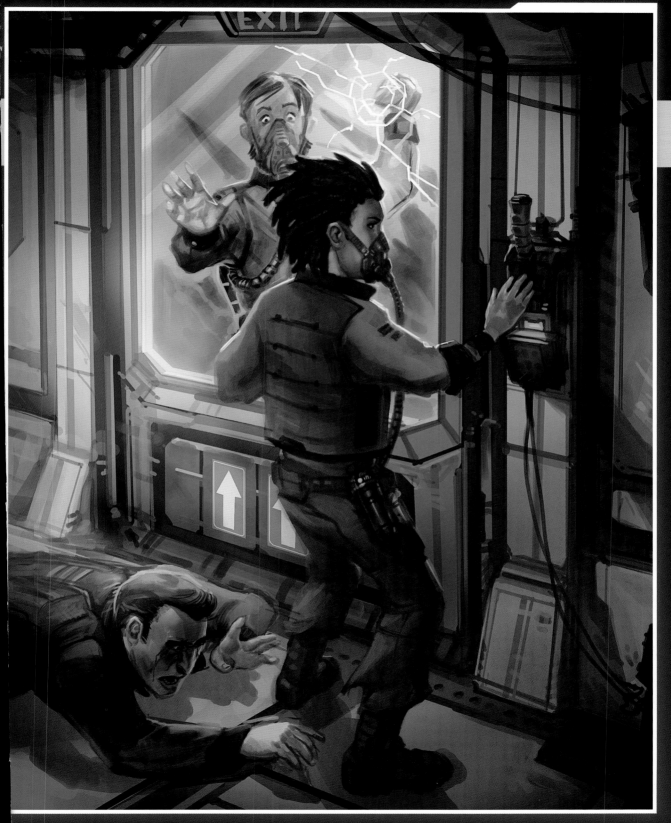

Boxer shrieked, the breather falling out of his mouth. In seconds he'd begin convulsing.

"So much for the hero always making it out alive," he said, as he yanked down the door access lever. Tremors ran through his muscles as the first convulsion hit, knocking him to his knees.

Through bleary eyes, he saw the scientists pour through the doorway.

As everything went black, Boxer just hoped he wouldn't eat them before they saved the world.

Curious clownfish out.
Colorful!

Closing time at the aquarium.
Let's go out!

Index

Websites to Visit

www.sheddaquarium.org/

www.montereybayaquarium.org/lc/activities/critter_cards.asp

animals.nationalgeographic.com/animals/fish/electric-eel.html

About the Authors

Thanks to phone calls and e-mails, Meg Greve and Luana Mitten can work together even though they live about 1,200 miles (1,900 kilometers) apart. Meg lives in the big city of Chicago, Illinois and gets to play in the snow with her kids. Luana lives on a golf course in Tampa, Florida and gets freckles on her face from playing at the beach with her son.

Artist: Madison Greve